Library of   Congress   Cataloging-in-
Publication Data: Chedru, Delphine. [La   petite bête qui monte.
English.] Spot it again! :   find more hidden creatures/   Delphine Chedru.   p. cm.
"Originally published in France in 2009 by Hélium under the title La petite bête qui monte."
ISBN 978-0-8109-9736-3 (alk. paper)   1. Picture puzzles—Juvenile literature.   I. Title.
GV1507.P47C4513 2011   793.73—dc22   2010020924
Copyright © 2009 Hélium Book design by: Les Associés reunis.
Translated from the French by Scott Auerbach
Originally published in France in 2009 by Hélium under the title *La petite bête qui monte*.
English edition published in 2011 by Abrams Books for Young Readers, an imprint of ABRAMS.

Printed and bound in Malaysia
10 9 8 7 6 5 4 3 2 1
Abrams Books for Young Readers are available at special discounts
when purchased in quantity for premiums and promotions as well
as fundraising or educational use. Special editions can also
be created to specification. For details, contact
specialmarkets@abramsbooks.com
or the address below.

ABRAMS
THE ART OF BOOKS SINCE 1949

115 West 18th Street, New York, NY 10011 • www.abramsbooks.com

SPOT IT AGAIN!

Find More Hidden Creatures

Delphine Chedru

Abrams Books for Young Readers, New York

Find the wandering caterpillar . . .

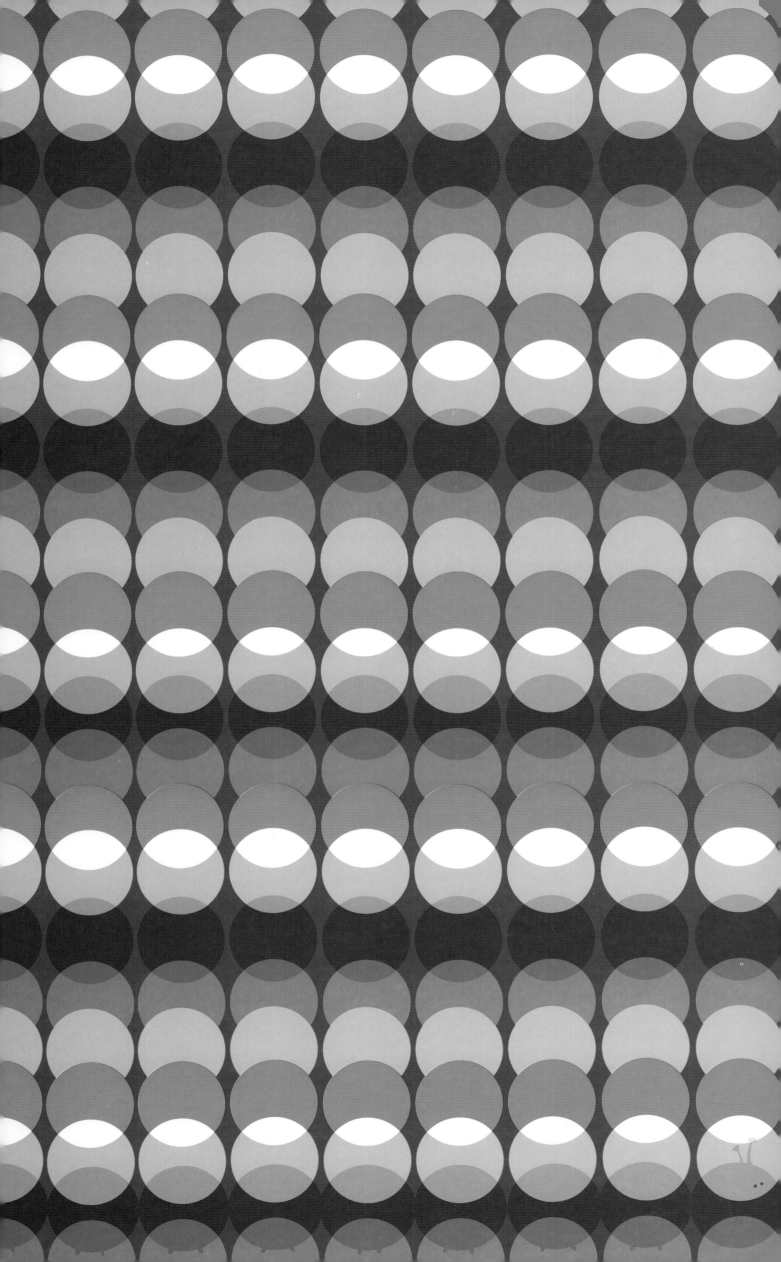

The earthworm with eyes bigger than his stomach . . .

The four-leaf clover . . .

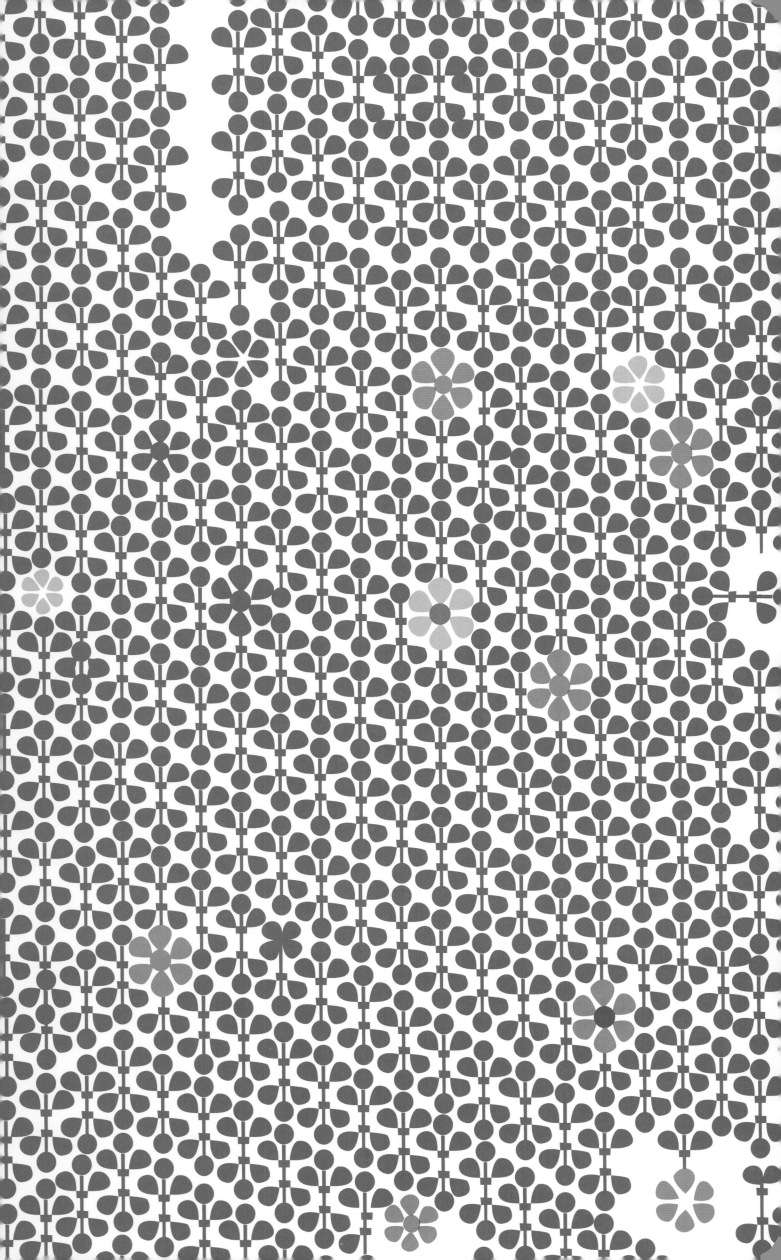

The chilly little spider . . .

The snake searching
for her baby . . .

The zebra who blends
in like a chameleon . . .

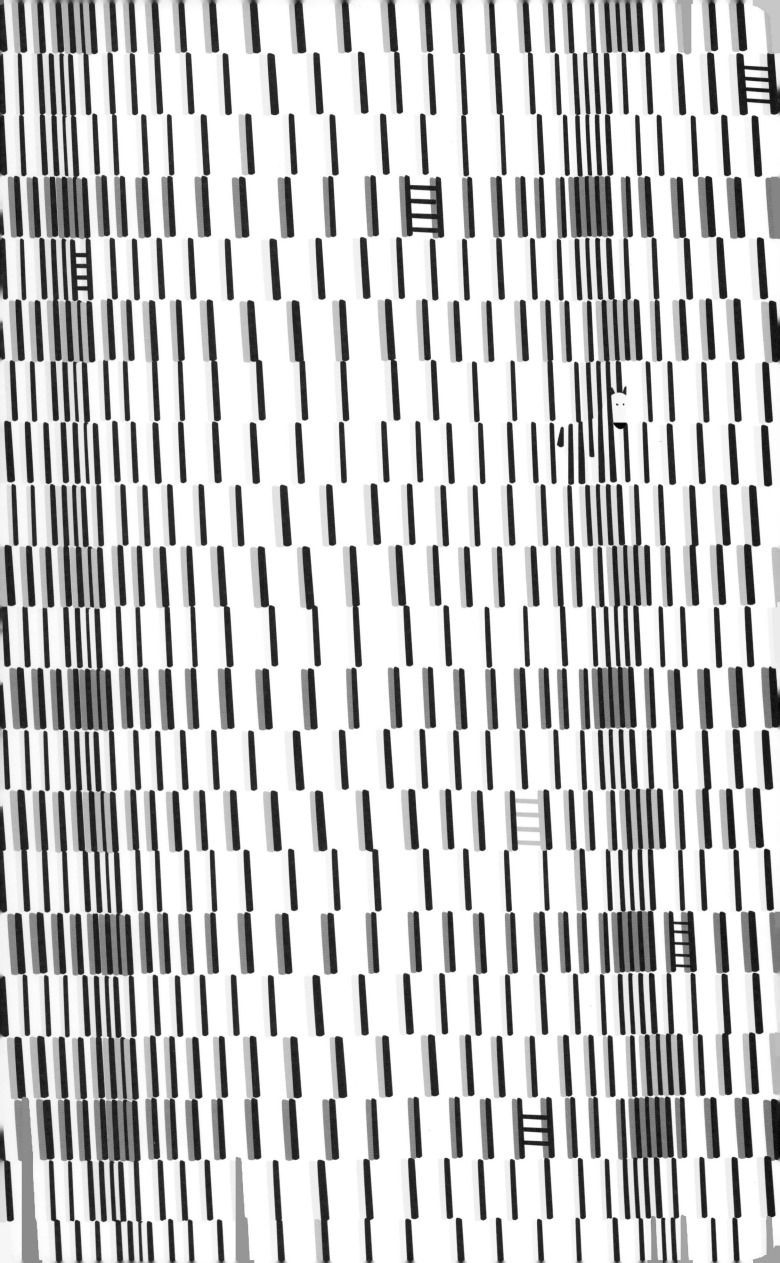

The walrus who's fond of a fan . . .

The starfish searching
for her little brother . . .

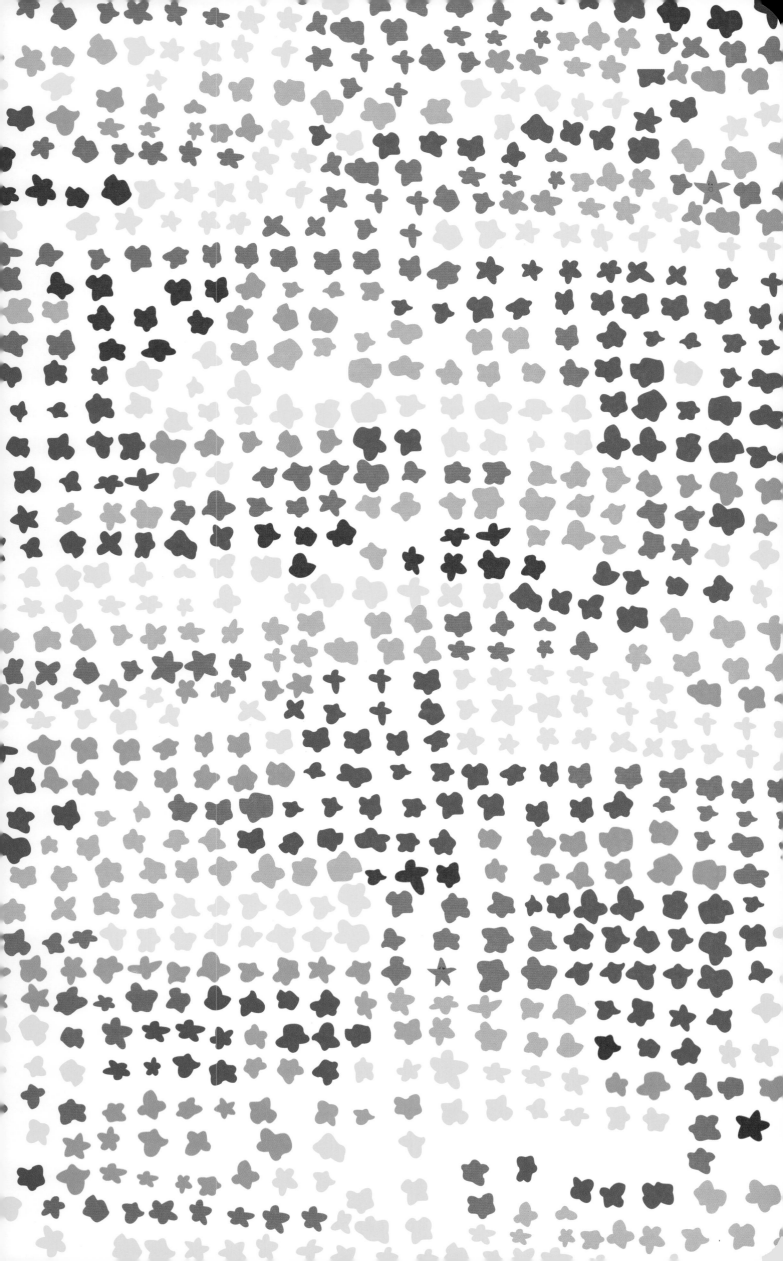

The koala who's green (with fright) . . .

. . . at the thought of being bitten
by the crying crocodile . . .

The flying fish . . .

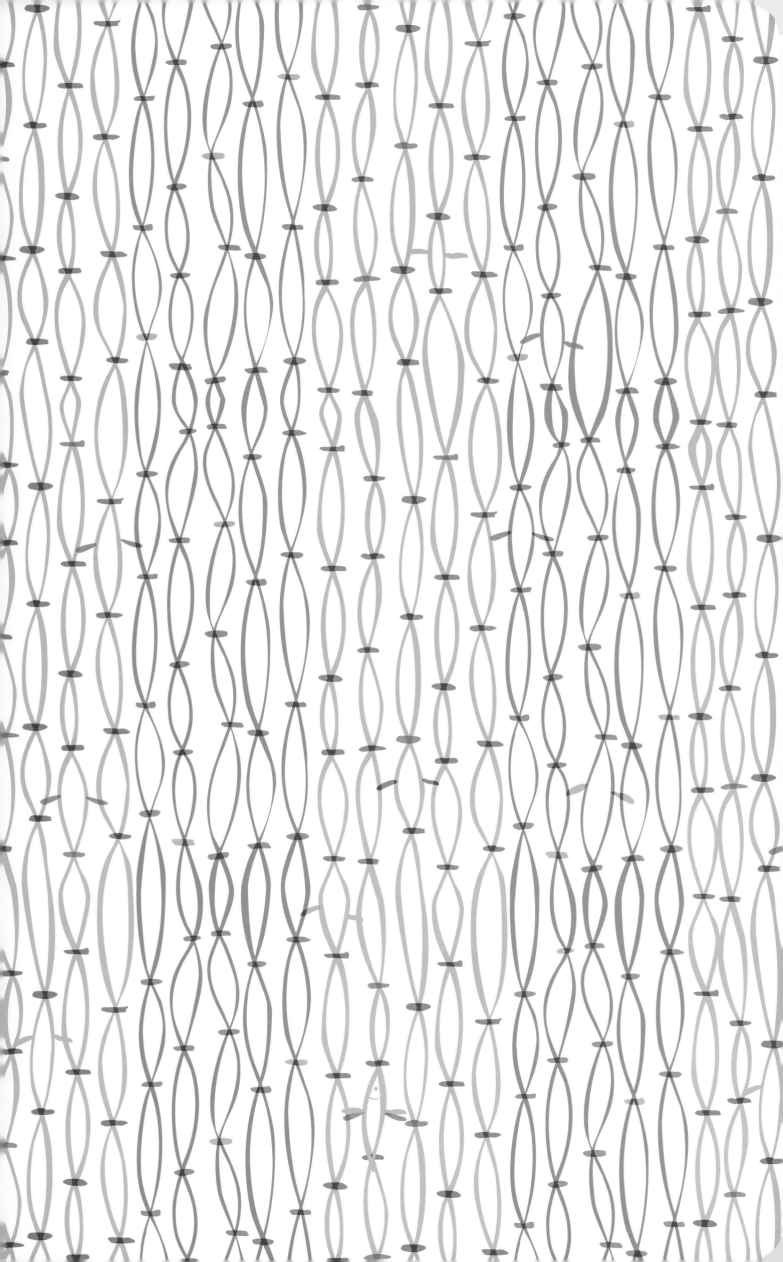

The snail and
his winged
friend . . .

The owl who just woke up . . .

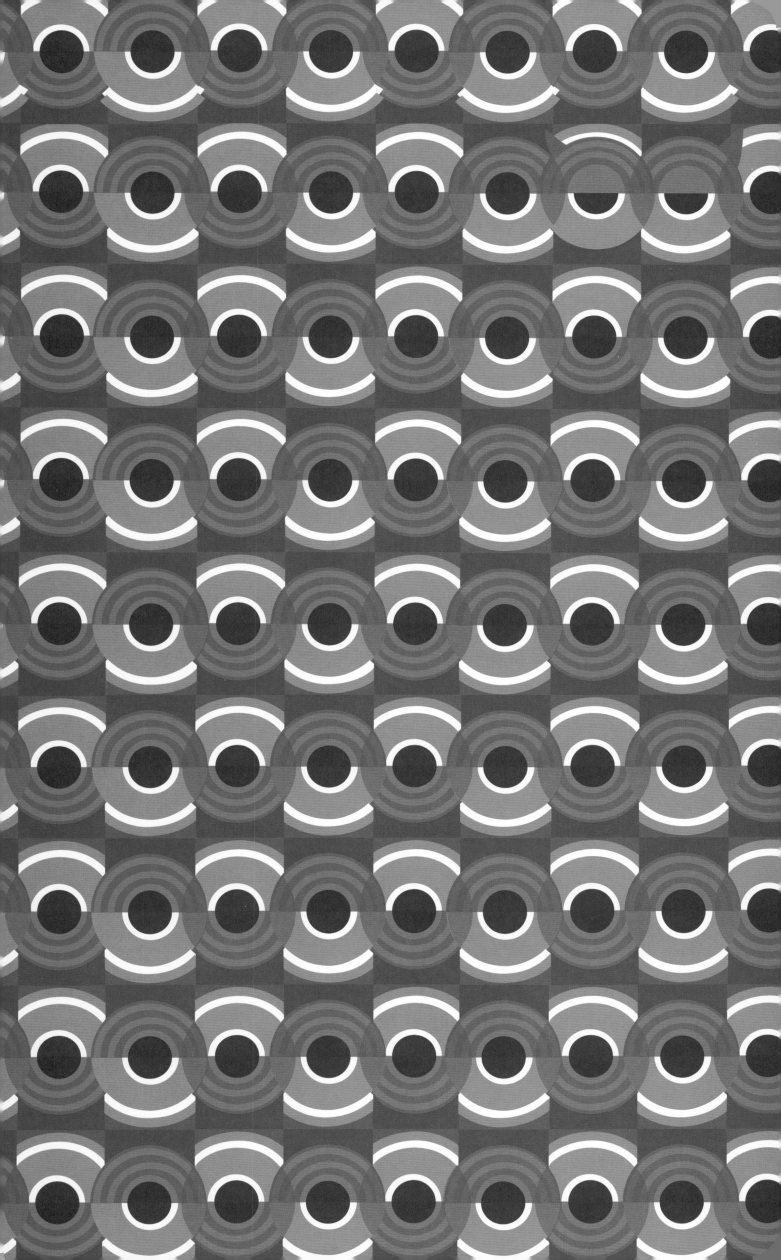

The world-champion
aphid . . .

And the penguin who's all wet because he forgot his raincoat.

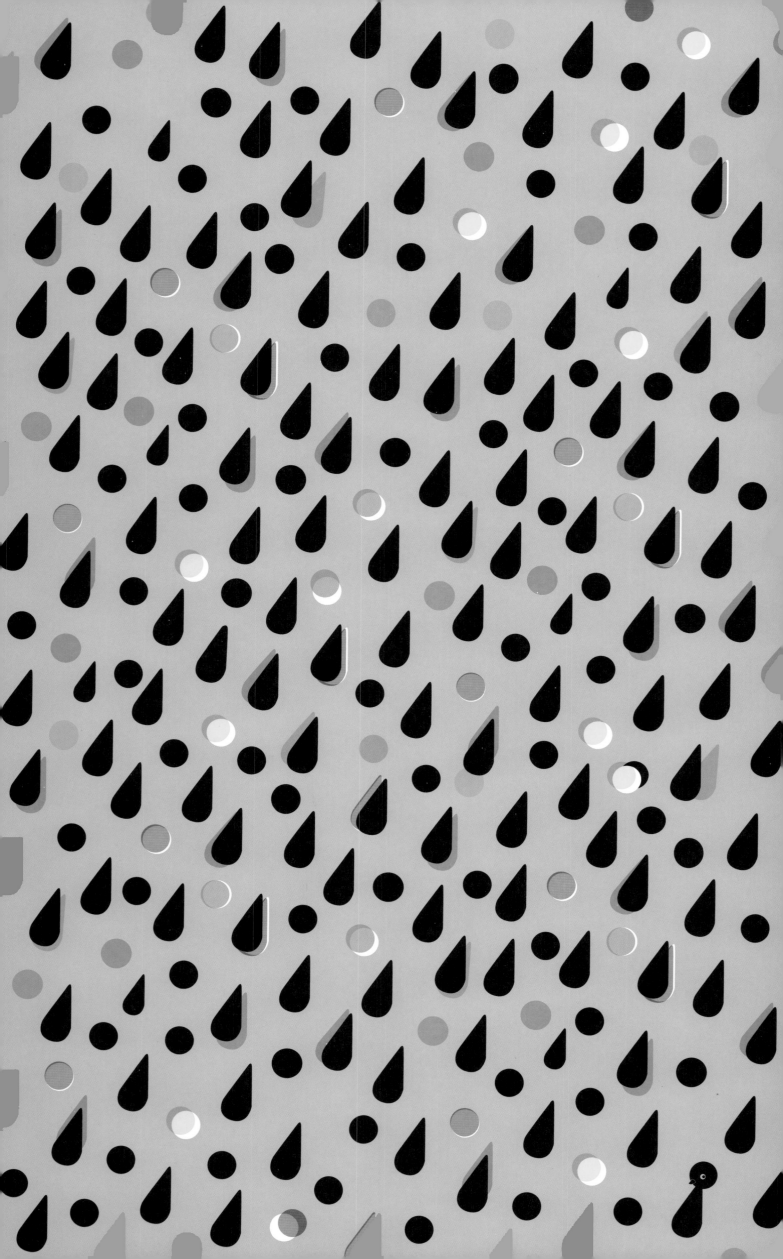

Night has fallen . . .

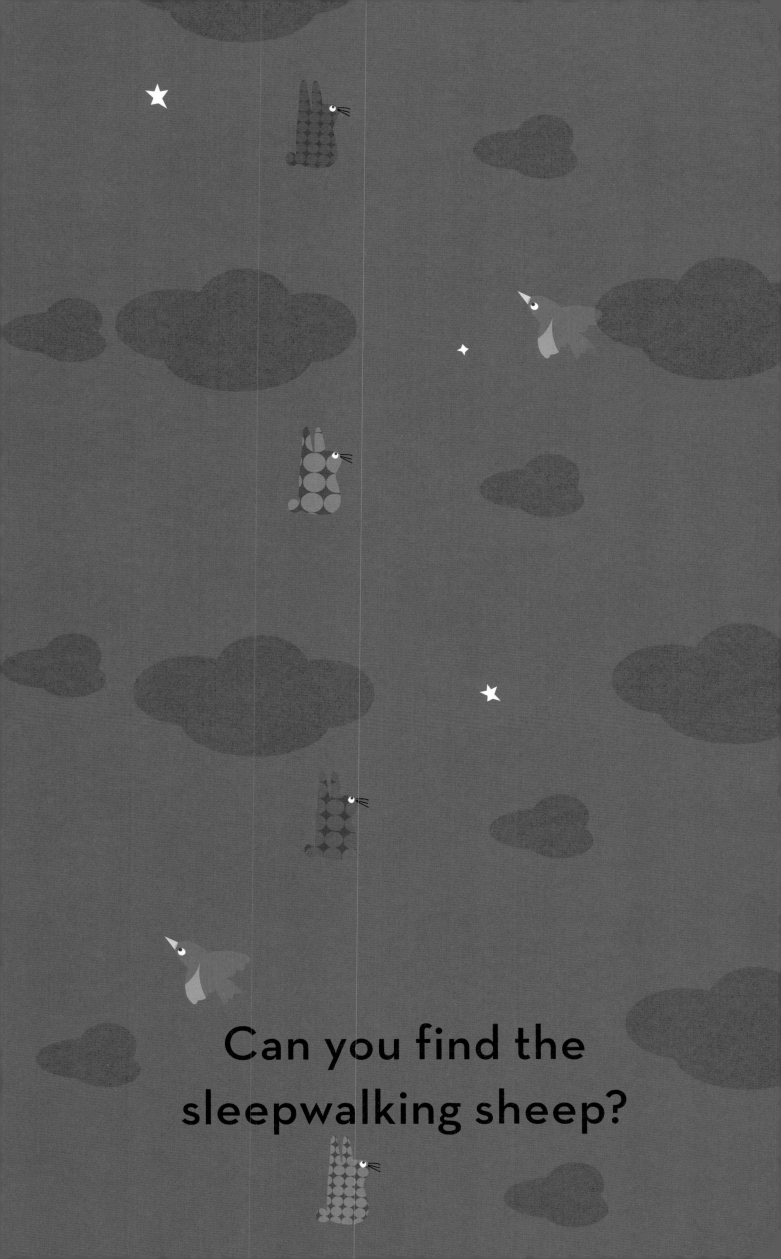

Can you find the
sleepwalking sheep?